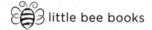 little bee books

New York, NY
Text copyright © 2022 by Cort Lane
Illustrations copyright © 2022 by Little Bee Books
All rights reserved, including the right of reproduction
in whole or in part in any form.
Library of Congress Cataloging-in-Publication Data
is available upon request.
For information about special discounts on bulk purchases,
please contact Little Bee Books at sales@littlebeebooks.com.
Manufactured in China   RRD 0322
ISBN 978-1-4998-1291-6 (paperback)
First Edition 10 9 8 7 6 5 4 3 2 1
ISBN 978-1-4998-1292-3 (hardcover)
First Edition 10 9 8 7 6 5 4 3 2 1
ISBN 978-1-4998-1293-0 (ebook)

littlebeebooks.com

MONSTER AND ME

WHO'S THE SCAREDY-CAT?

BY **CORT LANE**

ILLUSTRATED BY
ANKITHA KINI

🐝 little bee books

Contents

Chapter 1:
Brothers and Best Friends

"**W**AAHOOO!!!" Freddy von Frankenstein zoomed down the mountain in his brand-new, three-wheeled super-cycle! Like most of his favorite things, he had built it himself, and this was his first time taking it for a spin. He couldn't wait to zip over boulders and whoosh straight down the mountain's steep cliffs.

In the passenger seat, Freddy's big brother, F.M., held his stomach. "Can you slow down a bit, Freddy?" F.M. asked, but Freddy was going so fast F.M.'s pleas were lost in the wind.

"This is my best invention yet!" Freddy cried. "We're gonna have so much fun!"

It wasn't just the super speed of Freddy's super-cycle that scared F.M. He was afraid of A LOT of things: bees, clowns, spiders, thunder, scary movies, fire—you name it!

But he was most afraid of the people who lived in the village at the foot of the mountain. And it seemed that's right where Freddy was headed.

F.M. had never been to the village before. He and Freddy lived in Nepal, high up in the Himalaya Mountains, far away from most people.

Their dad, Victor, had moved to the mountains to keep F.M. safe from humans. Victor von Frankenstein was one of the world's most brilliant scientists, and F.M. was his greatest invention.

Nine years ago, Victor made F.M. in a laboratory in Europe. He used machines and chemicals, and even lightning! And one night, F.M. was alive! Victor loved F.M., but the townspeople took one look at his huge size and gray skin, and were afraid. Their fear made them unkind. They chased him with torches and called him "Frankenstein's Monster."

F.M. didn't like being called a monster at first. He knew monsters were scary and mean, and he was very, very kind. Over time, he decided that being a "monster" meant that he was unique, and he didn't mind the name so much. But he never forgot how scary and mean the townspeople were to him, and from then on, he was afraid of humans. So Victor found a place where there were no humans around to frighten F.M.

Freddy loved having F.M. as a big brother!

Just some reasons why it's so cool:

F.M. gives the best piggyback rides.

He can reach stuff in high places.

He can throw Freddy in the lake.

He can carry all
of Freddy's inventions
when they conk out.

And he can carry
Freddy when HE conks
out after a long day of
adventures.

He's superstrong and can't
be hurt, even if his huge
hands and feet can make
him a little clumsy.

Who wouldn't want an awesome brother like that?

Chapter 2:
The Monster's Mix-Up

"I can't believe we finally get to explore on our own!" Freddy said excitedly. It was his first trip to town without his mom and dad.

"I just hope the people there aren't scared of me," F.M. said.

Freddy thought about how much he loved his big brother. He wished other people could see how great F.M. was.

"I have an idea," Freddy said. "If we meet a villager, let's introduce ourselves. Maybe we'll make some friends!"

But the look on F.M.'s face told Freddy that today was not the day to try new things.

"Have no fear!" Freddy said cheerfully. "I'll make you a disguise." He parked the super-cycle and whipped out a high-tech device and pointed it at F.M.

"This won't hurt at all. Right, Freddy?" F.M. asked suspiciously.

"No way! This ray will only project a hologram so that you can appear completely disguised to anyone looking at you. I call it . . . the Disguise-o-Tron! But here, you have to wear this wristband."

Freddy snapped a metal wristband on F.M.'s arm and then fired the ray at him. Bright light surrounded him until suddenly, the hologram projection changed F.M. from a monster to just looking like Freddy's very normal big brother with an *extra* tall hat on his head.

The robotic arms from his high-tech backpack put the invention away.

F.M. caught his reflection in the super-cycle. "Wow, this might actually work!" F.M. exclaimed. "Thanks, Freddy!"

The two of them headed down the slope and into town. Houses both big and small were on either side. People passing by greeted Freddy and F.M., smiling and saying, "Namaste."

"Namaste," they said back to the villagers with a wave. Eventually, the brothers found themselves at a big, outdoor market.

"Wow! Look at all the awesome stuff they have!" Freddy shouted. He zipped off to a stand full of flags.

F.M. looked around at all the stalls. He had a secret reason for wanting to go into town that he didn't tell Freddy—their mom asked him to shop for Freddy's surprise eighth-birthday party! So when Freddy wasn't looking, F.M. sneaked around shopping for decorations and surprises for tomorrow's party. He found streamers, noisemakers, silly hats, and candles for the cake!

After F.M. bought all he needed and hid it in his backpack, Freddy came rushing back with his bag, filled to the brim with local crafts.

"I got so many cool—" Freddy was so excited that he ran *right* into F.M.'s arm, and the wristband—and F.M.'s disguise—suddenly turned off. One by one, the shocked shoppers turned to see F.M. in his true form!

"Ahhhhh!" F.M. shouted and ran away from the humans. The shopkeeper started to run after him, but F.M. was already halfway out of town.

"I only wanted to give him his change," the shopkeeper said to Freddy.

"Thanks!" Freddy said, and laughed all the way through town as he followed F.M. back to the super-cycle.

Chapter 3:
Freddy Freaks Out

Freddy and F.M. zoomed toward home on their super-cycle as it started to get dark.

"I don't know why you're still scared of people. It's usually humans that are afraid of monsters, and only sometimes! I mean, the shopkeeper wasn't even scared of you!" Freddy said. "And I'm not scared of monsters at all, big brother."

F.M. just wanted to get home, so he didn't complain during the fast, bumpy ride. The super-cycle raced across rocks, a river, and snow as they quickly climbed to the top of their mountain. F.M. was annoyed as tree branches kept smacking his face. Freddy giggled as his brother shouted, "Ow!" and "Oof!"

"Maybe you need to invent a tree guard to protect me from the branches," F.M. moaned.

As they neared the palace, Freddy suddenly slammed on the brakes.

"What is it?" F.M. asked. Freddy pointed to a dark figure in the middle of their path. The shadow stepped forward, and it was a tiger! Or something that looked like it.

"Ahh! It's some kind of evil tiger monster!" Freddy shouted.

"It doesn't look very monstrous to me," F.M. whispered.

"Well, you've never seen a tiger in real life! Maybe it's just a regular tiger," F.M. whispered.

Freddy said, "I've seen plenty of tigers in books and they don't look like that!"

The creature's eyes seemed to glow magically, and it let out a sharp growl. *Now I'm pretty sure it's a monster!* Freddy thought.

"Hello, pretty kitty," F.M. called, unafraid. The creature growled even louder!

"That's it, I'm outta here." Freddy turned the super-cycle clumsily, pushed the speed button, and zoomed off toward home. His fast turn bumped the super-cycle into some boulders, denting it before it climbed up the mountain at top speed. Freddy yelped at the bumps and F.M. held on tight.

"Maybe you ARE afraid of monsters, after all," said F.M.

"Hey, I'm not scared of anything scientific. But it doesn't look like anything made by science, like you were. It's not the same!" Freddy shot back. "I'm kind of surprised you weren't scared by it."

Freddy rounded a curve, and their home came into view.

"I guess I thought it just seemed more scared of us than we were of it," F.M. said.

Suddenly, a roar rang out in the distance. It sounded even bigger and worse than that tiger! The roar got louder and echoed through the mountains.

"What was *that*?!" F.M. asked.

"Let's not wait around to find out," Freddy shouted, and they hopped off the super-cycle and ran inside the palace, locking the door behind them!

Chapter 4:
Lucky Number Eight

The next morning, F.M. was up early, happily putting the finishing touches on Freddy's birthday gifts. He wrapped the presents with paper and ribbons and got the decorations ready. But with his huge, clumsy hands, he mostly made a funny-looking mess.

When Freddy finally woke up and tried to get into F.M.'s room, his brother frantically shut the door to hide all the party surprises.

"Uhh, don't come in yet!" F.M. shouted through the door. "But hey, happy birthday! Eight is going to be your lucky number!"

Freddy responded, "Hmm, I thought seven was going to be my lucky number, but nothing all that special happened."

F.M. reminded him, "Mom always says eight is a very lucky number. And well . . . Mom is right about everything." F.M. sneaked out of his room and slammed the door before Freddy could peek inside. "Let's go find Mom and ask her what a lucky eighth birthday is like. I bet she will have some fun ideas for your party today."

Freddy, always excited to talk about his birthday, dragged his brother through the palace. They walked through the colorful, twisty hallways of their home.

When Victor's search to find a new home for F.M. took them to China, Victor met and fell in love with Freddy's mom, Shan. Shan loved F.M. like her own son, and she helped them find this beautiful old palace in Nepal. She knew it was a perfect place both for F.M. to live safely and for Victor to do his experiments.

The Palace of the High Winds was here long before the Frankensteins moved in. It had been covered by snow for centuries, but Victor's amazing snow-melting ray uncovered it. It's full of winding stairs, painted carvings, and in the middle is a huge

room that Victor turned into a giant laboratory. The lab had lots of machines, tubes, and wires running all across it and up to the ceiling. And the roof even slid open so Victor could use lightning to power his experiments!

Freddy and F.M. walked up to their dad's lab. When Victor was running crazy experiments, the door was usually shut for their safety. Sometimes, Victor's inventions would mess up—like the time Victor tried to invent a machine to turn broccoli into milkshakes but only managed to create clouds of green smoke that shot out from underneath the door. Or that other time when  he came out covered in purple goo from a flying bubble that popped when he was floating in it.

 Freddy learned from his dad that being a genius can be very messy, but mistakes are just part of being a great scientist. Victor simply shrugged when something went wrong and tried again and again until he got it right.

But on that day, the door to the lab was open, and Freddy heard his parents talking to someone.

"Who could that be?" Freddy asked. "We never have visitors!"

F.M. shrugged and Victor waved them in. There was a shy, young girl dressed in a salwar kameez standing in front of them. Shan said, "Boys, I'd like you to meet Riya. She's not from the town below, but actually came all the way from her village in northern India." Victor added, "She is tired and alone, with no place to go, so she's going to stay with us for a while."

Freddy looked to F.M. for his reaction, but his brother was hiding. F.M. was scared of any strange human. Her story didn't make sense to Freddy at all. So he marched up to her and started asking a bunch of questions.

"How did you get here?" Freddy asked, eyeing her suspiciously.

"I walked a long, long way," Riya said.

Freddy couldn't imagine how she could do that. "Why did you leave India?"

"I have no family, and the people there wanted me to leave," said Riya, looking sad.

Freddy noticed his mom giving him her I'm-disappointed-in-how-rude-you're-being look. So he asked a nicer question, "How old are you?"

"Eleven," said Riya.

Hmm, older kids are bossy, thought Freddy.

"Well, what's your favorite dinosaur?"

"I—I don't know," she said.

"You don't have a favorite dinosaur?!" Freddy was shocked. *How can you trust someone who doesn't even like dinosaurs?* he thought.

"Why did the people in India want you to leave?"
Riya looked down and didn't speak.

"Be friendly, Freddy!" Shan scolded. "This palace has made room for us, and there is plenty of space for guests in need like Riya. Freddy, please set up a room for her. You are welcome to stay as long as you wish, Riya."

Freddy's jaw dropped. *Ugh, why did this have to happen today—MY BIRTHDAY! Now, the day will be all about this girl.*

"Listen to your mother, Freddy," said Victor.

F.M. came out from his hiding spot and asked, "I know what it's like to have people chase you away. Were you scared when you finally ran off?"

Riya raised her eyebrows in shock at seeing F.M., but replied, "I'll tell you another time. I'm a bit tired from climbing the mountain."

Freddy reluctantly took her to an empty room upstairs with a soft, comfy bed. The bedroom was draped with beautiful fabrics that were made in town.

"Thank you, it looks so lovely and cozy," Riya said, smiling with relief.

"Well, at least you're happy," complained Freddy. "Today was supposed to be all about my birthday. But now I guess we need to take care of you."

Riya looked surprised and replied, "I'm so sorry. I don't want to spoil anyone's birthday!"

Freddy just grumbled and said, "Come on, let's get you some breakfast."

Chapter 5:
Igor's Plan

Inside the kitchen, a golden langur monkey was staring up at a giant cake high up on a shelf. He had bright orange fur and a coal-colored face that looked grumpy, but he wasn't grumpy at that moment—he was hungry! Igor was the pet monkey of the palace, living there as long as Freddy could remember.

The sneaky monkey climbed the cabinets and stretched as far as he could until the cake was almost within reach. Suddenly, he knocked down a whole mess of pots and pans that fell right on his head. Freddy and Riya rushed in at the noise.

"Igor! You naughty monkey!" Freddy shouted. But Igor wasn't listening, he was looking up at the glorious, giant cake about to fall right on top of him! Just then, Riya jumped quickly across the room and gracefully caught the cake.

"I've known many monkeys like you, Igor, always causing mischief," Riya scolded him. Her eyes seemed to glow at the monkey. Igor slid away sideways with a guilty grin.

How could she move that fast? Freddy wondered. *And what was that glow in her eyes?*

Behind him, Shan walked in and laughed at Igor's disappointment. Shan said, "You're going to fit in just fine here, Riya. Would you like some breakfast?"

Oh, no! Freddy thought. *If she fits in so well here, she'll never leave.*

After breakfast, Freddy moped around the palace. With everyone helping Riya, he was sure they wouldn't give much thought to his birthday.

Where is everyone? He wondered.

He wandered back into the kitchen and found F.M. making a mountain of grilled cheese sandwiches. Freddy loved grilled cheese sandwiches, but he was feeling grumpy. "I hope those aren't for me," he snapped. "Grilled cheese sandwiches are your favorite, not mine."

F.M. turned to their mom, who was standing nearby. "Ever since Riya arrived, Freddy has been acting different," he whispered. "I know he really loves grilled cheese almost as much as I do!"

Freddy also noticed Riya over in the corner, who seemed to be trying to hide what she was making. Freddy watched her suspiciously and thought, *Just another reason to not like having this girl around.*

"What are you making?" Freddy asked, trying to see around her.

"Nothing! Don't worry about it!" Riya covered a pot filled with food she had prepared. She rushed out of the room with the pot in her arms.

That's even more strange, thought Freddy. *What is she hiding now? She's as sneaky as Igor!*

"Oh, Freddy!" Victor called from the lab. "Come see your birthday present!" Freddy shot out of the kitchen with F.M. close behind.

"Ta-da!" Victor had fixed the dent in Freddy's super-cycle! "Just like new," he said. "And I added a jet-powered turbo boost!"

"No way! This is awesome. Thanks so much, Dad!" Freddy yelled with excitement. "I can't wait to try it out at top speed! We gotta go ride it now!" he said to F.M.

F.M. held his stomach, already anticipating getting carsick from the speed boost.

"Maybe you can do that after dinner," Shan said to F.M.'s relief. "We have somebody's birthday to celebrate, remember?"

Freddy was pleased that she hadn't forgotten even with Riya around. *Though where did Riya sneak off to?* he wondered.

ROARRR!

A giant, menacing roar came from upstairs and echoed all through the halls of the palace. Freddy and F.M. looked at each other, both thinking the same thing—it must be the same creature they saw last night!

Everyone ran to the staircase to see what was going on.

"There it is!" Freddy shouted. The tiger beast from yesterday was running down the stairs that led to Riya's room—and it was coming right at him!

Chapter 6:
A Monster Mystery

The tiger was almost upon Freddy. It leapt through the air right at him and he closed his eyes and waited for the worst to happen. But it jumped over him and then crashed through the front door. Freddy and his parents watched the tiger run away until it disappeared. Igor was shaking, hanging from a wooden beam in the ceiling with his tail. F.M. hurried up to Riya's room—she was missing, too!

"Did Riya somehow escape from the creature?" F.M. asked.

"That tiger looked oddly . . . human-like," Victor remarked, stroking his chin.

Shan and Victor looked at each other worriedly. Freddy was surprised that he felt sad for Riya, especially if she was as afraid of the tiger as he was. *Not that I was actually scared of it or anything*, he thought to himself.

After searching the whole house, they couldn't find Riya anywhere. Shan was worried. "Oh, no! Where is that poor girl?"

Victor announced, "I have special inventions that can search across the mountain for her, but it will take some time to power them up."

F.M. wondered, "What if she is in danger now? Or scared and lost? I'll go outside to search for Riya." Even though he was still afraid of her and that tiger, F.M. was determined to help. "I'm the best one to save her because a tiger is no threat to me with my strength and toughness."

Inspired by his brother's bravery, Freddy also offered to help. "I'll go, too!" Freddy said. "The search will go much faster if I drive you on my super-cycle and use my own inventions."

Their mom and dad were worried about their boys being in danger. But they agreed to let them go as long as F.M. promised to keep his brother safe.

Yes! Freddy thought, hoping he would finally have the kind of big adventure he'd always wanted. He brought F.M. some of those grilled cheese sandwiches as supplies. Adventures usually made both of them hungry.

Freddy and F.M. took off driving across the mountaintop to look for Riya. Freddy put on a pair of high-tech goggles. "These will help me track the tiger paw prints! But weirdly, they're not picking up any human footprints from Riya."

Freddy hit the button to start up the turbo boost his dad added. *ZOOM!* They suddenly rocketed off three times faster than before!

"Yeah!" Freddy shouted with delight.

"Aaaaaaaaaaa!" F.M. cried in terror.

Freddy flipped a switch on his goggles, changing from tracking paw prints to the infrared setting that allowed him to see things that are hot and cold. The goggles' infrared vision could help him see someone's body heat from a mile away. Using them now, he could see something warm not too far ahead, so he drove toward it. *Could it be the creature or Riya?* he wondered. As the sky grew dark, they started to get closer to whatever it was, and Freddy slowed down the super-cycle.

"Riya?" F.M. called gently. Suddenly, the ferocious-looking tiger creature stepped out of the shadows, its orange fur shining in the moonlight.

Freddy looked warily at its long claws and sharp teeth. *Did this creature have something to do with Riya's disappearance?* he wondered. Freddy shook with fear. "Back up, F.M.!"

But F.M. called out calmly, "Here, kitty, kitty! It's okay." The tiger started backing up, but then everything grew darker as a cloud covered the moon. Freddy and F.M. watched with surprise as the creature started to change shape—and turned right into Riya!

Chapter 7:
Riya's Story

"**W**hat the . . . how the . . . what?!" Freddy exclaimed in shock. Riya looked scared and said nothing.

F.M. asked her, "Are you a monster girl or a human girl?"

Riya sighed and said, "Both . . . I was frightened you wouldn't accept me if you knew the truth."

"You're *both*?" Freddy asked.

"Yes."

After a pause, F.M. asked, "And you didn't think we'd accept you because of that?"

Riya explained, "I have the magical curse of the werecat. That means magic turns me from a human into a tiger creature when the moon is full. I can't control it. My village was so scared of me, they ran me right out of town. Without any family to help, I ran far away and ended up here." Riya looked sad and embarrassed.

"I understand how you feel. The same thing happened to me," F.M. said. "Humans were afraid of me and chased me away, too. That's why Dad brought me to this mountain, where no one was around to be afraid of me." F.M. announced happily, "Well, you can stay on this mountain with us and never be afraid of people again! Right, Freddy?"

Freddy wasn't so sure. "I don't like the sound of this 'curse.' I can't be cursed, too, just by helping you, right?"

But what Freddy was really worried about was her moving in with them. *I don't want anyone messing up the fun times with my brother,* he thought. *And she'll take up all of Mom and Dad's attention, too. I thought I wanted my life to have exciting adventures, but now this adventure has changed everything. I liked our family just the way it was.*

Riya looked down. "I don't think you can catch my curse. But then again, no one has helped me before, so I don't know."

Freddy felt bad for her. *On the other hand, now that I know the tiger creature is her and isn't dangerous, she's not THAT bad,* he thought. *And even though she ruined my birthday, she looks so afraid and lonely. . . .*

"Okay, hop on the super-cycle. We'll take you home. Are you okay to walk, F.M.? I guess I'll have to make some modifications to this to make more seats now that you're staying with us, Riya," said Freddy. F.M. nodded, and Riya smiled.

Just then, they heard the same loud, menacing roar that they heard yesterday!

"Whoa! Is there a second werecat?!" Freddy asked.

"Not that I know of!" Riya said, looking worried. Freddy put on his goggles again and scanned the mountain.

"There it is!" he shouted. A monster was lumbering up the mountain in their direction! It must have been twelve feet tall with long, white fur and giant claws.

"I can't believe it . . . it must be a yeti!" he said to F.M. and Riya. He had read the legends about yetis—giant, hairy monsters that lived in the Himalayas.

How can they be real? he thought. The massive monster roared again angrily, but this time, much closer to them.

Chapter 8:
The Yeti!

Freddy, F.M., and Riya looked on in shock. Freddy's goggles zoomed in and he could see that the yeti had long, sharp teeth! But it wasn't looking at them. It was climbing the mountain and going after something else.

"My goggles can see a campsite of human hikers not far from the yeti. They look like they're in danger!" Freddy could see the campers shouting and trembling with fear.

"Why is the yeti here?" F.M. asked, a little excited about meeting another monster. He was amazed they hadn't seen one in all these years. And today they'd seen two!

"The yeti might be here for the same reason I came to this mountain. I could feel it was a safe place for mystical creatures like me. Whatever that magical signal is, it must have attracted the yeti, too!" Riya said.

"Magical signal?" Freddy asked. "Doubtful. I've never heard of anything like that! There's no such thing as magic."

"I believe her," F.M. said. "That explains why she came all this way to our mountain. Why else would she have been drawn here, the middle of nowhere?"

F.M. sprang into action, running down the mountain to help the campers. Freddy was frozen in place, though. He was terrified and just wanted to zoom back home.

"We have to help F.M. and the campers!" Riya shouted.

Wow! She is so brave, thought Freddy. *If she can be brave, maybe I can, too.*

Freddy gunned the super-cycle and followed after F.M. to find him leaping in the snow. F.M. was trying to avoid the yeti as it was now chasing him. Freddy gulped. *Geez, this yeti's claws and teeth are even sharper up close*, he thought. *Wait a second . . . it keeps looking at F.M.'s backpack—which is full of those grilled cheese sandwiches!*

Suddenly, the clouds parted away from the moon, and Riya changed back to her tiger form. The yeti stopped chasing F.M. and stared at Riya in shock. The yeti let out a confused growl. "Grrrrrr?"

Riya roared and leapt in front of the yeti. She rolled into the yeti in an epic tumble.

Riya's attack gave Freddy just enough time to calm down and think. *I can't let my fear stop me from helping Riya, and those other people, and especially my brother.* He concentrated hard,

trying to think of a plan. *Even the supernatural is no match for my scientific brain!*

His backpack's robot arms handed him a bunch of tools. Freddy pulled off the turbo parts his dad

put on his super-cycle and whipped up a new invention as fast as he could. Meanwhile, F.M. and Riya were busy working as a team to distract the charging yeti.

"I'm ready!" Freddy announced.

Freddy revealed a shiny, high-tech sandwich cannon.

"Throw me some of those birthday grilled cheese sandwiches!" he shouted at his brother. F.M. reached into his backpack and tossed all of them right at Freddy. The yeti's eyes grew big as it saw sandwiches flying by, and it lunged. Freddy quickly stuffed the sandwiches into the cannon.

Freddy shot the grilled cheeses far away, over to the next mountain. The yeti turned around and ran off to chase after them.

"Yes!" Freddy yelled with delight.

Riya and F.M. came over and high-fived Freddy.

"That was awesome!" cried F.M.

"That was pretty cool," Riya added. Freddy marveled that she could even speak in her tiger form.

They all collapsed to the ground, relieved and happy. Freddy smiled and laughed. *That was my most epic adventure ever!*

Chapter 9:
Fantasticals

Riya squinted and used her tiger vision to look around the mountains. "I can see the yeti walking away with a belly full of grilled cheese. And all the hikers are safe, too."

"Wow, your tiger powers sure come in handy!" F.M. said, impressed.

"Hey, my goggles work just as well! Supernatural creatures are still no match for science!" Freddy argued. F.M. and Riya looked at each other and giggled, rolling their eyes at Freddy's boast.

F.M. gently reminded him, "You sure seemed scared of that monster at first."

"Monsters that can't be explained by science, I'll never understand. Magical beasts are scary." Riya looked down.

"Well, Riya is a fantastical creature, and she's not scary at all," said F.M.

"Thank you," said Riya, flashing a smile.

"That's true. I didn't mean to hurt your feelings, Riya," Freddy said. "Fantastical, I like that. Instead of calling you a monster, we'll call you a fantastical!"

"I hope we get to meet more fantasticals!" cheered F.M., putting his big, gentle hands on both of their shoulders. "Let's go home."

Back at the palace, Victor and Shan gave each of them a hug in relief.

Freddy began to excitedly tell them about everything that happened. "We found the tiger creature, and it was Riya! You see, she has a werecat curse and changes when the moon is full. That's why she had to leave her village. But then clouds came, and she turned back into a human!"

Victor smiled and said, "Well, it's a good thing you boys found her and brought her back to us. Now, let's check all of you out."

Then Freddy shouted, "But that's not all, Dad! We saw an actual yeti climbing up the mountain. And . . . and . . ." Freddy had to take a deep breath. Victor and Shan's eyes were huge, listening to the tale of the yeti. Before F.M. could add anything, Freddy kept talking as fast as he could.

"There were campers in danger, so we had to stop the yeti! Riya turned back into a tiger creature, and she and F.M. distracted it! Then I invented a grilled cheese cannon right then and there to trick the yeti into leaving—it was amazing! And we don't call Riya a monster because we've decided to call her a fantastical."

"She's pretty fantastic, after all!" added F.M., excited to get a chance to speak.

Victor and Shan were moved listening to Riya's story. Shan declared, "You can live with us as a part of our family!"

Riya wiped away a tear. "Thank you, I've never really had a family before."

Later on, as the brothers put the super-cycle away, F.M. said, "It will be so cool to have an older sister."

Freddy nodded, but didn't look happy. "Riya is older, has really cool powers for Dad to study, and seems to already get along really well with Mom, too," Freddy worried.

F.M. put his hands on his little brother's shoulders and guided him through the palace's twisty halls.

"It will be different having a new sibling, but that doesn't mean it can't be fun," F.M. reassured Freddy. "Didn't Dad create a turbo boost for your super-cycle today, while Riya was already here? And Mom has enough love in her heart for two of us. So why not three? Besides, you will always be MY best friend, no matter what. I'd bet a hundred grilled cheese sandwiches you don't need to be afraid of having a sister. Look!"

Just then, F.M. threw open the doors to Dad's laboratory.

Chapter 10:
Surprise!

Riya, Mom, Dad, and F.M. yelled, "Surprise!" as Freddy walked in. Even Igor was there for his birthday party—probably because there was cake. Freddy looked around and saw there were presents! There were also messy decorations made by F.M.! And there was a big feast for dinner! F.M. shouted, "Yaaaaaaay!" He jumped up and down with excitement, making the room shake. Freddy laughed to see a terrified Igor stuck on top of a balloon, floating up to the ceiling!

Riya came up to him. "I made this for you. It's called laddoo, an Indian treat. They're sweet little balls, like doughnuts. Back home, it's a birthday tradition to eat them BEFORE dinner!"

Dessert before dinner? Yum! thought Freddy. *And wait, this must be the mysterious food Riya was making earlier!*

"Thank you so much, Riya!" Freddy smiled. *Maybe having a big sister might be kind of cool.*

For dinner, Freddy's mom had made longevity noodles. Freddy explained to Riya, "It's good luck to eat the long noodles without breaking them." Everyone slurped them up carefully.

After dinner, Shan gave Freddy a big hug. "The noodles aren't the only lucky thing on your birthday. Eight is the *luckiest* number of all! And today proves it—it was a lucky day for you, Riya, and the people you saved, too."

Freddy rolled his eyes and said, "I don't know about silly magic stuff like luck. I just believe in science." But Shan reminded him, "You already helped a werecat *and* a yeti today. That's proof that magic is real. So luck must be real as well."

Before Freddy could argue, Victor and Riya interrupted, marching in with the giant cake! F.M. gasped with glee. Igor drooled at the sight of it.

Victor said, "This is the perfect chance to try out my new laser multi-candle lighter!" He pressed a button, and his invention shot out eight tiny laser beams to set all the candles on fire. But F.M., suddenly remembering how terrified of flames he was, ran away—right through the nearest wall! Freddy laughed at the monster-shaped hole F.M. left in the wall.

Victor sighed. "I know I have a wall-repairing machine somewhere. Now where did I put that thing?"

Shan, trying not to laugh, shook her head at both F.M. and her husband. "Time to make a wish, Freddy."

Freddy thought it over. *I wish to have more exciting adventures like today—though maybe with not quite as many fantasticals.* And he blew out the candles.

As he looked back and giggled at the giant hole in the wall, he saw Riya giggling, too. *Having a big sister will be very different,* thought Freddy. *But just because something is different doesn't mean I should be scared of it.* Freddy looked up at his mom and said, "It ended up being a pretty awesome birthday after all!"

MONKEY MISCHIEF

SPLAT!

Journey to some magical places and outer space, rock out, and find your inner superhero with these other chapter book series from Little Bee Books!

Tales of SASHA

#1

The Big Secret

by Alexa Pearl
Illustrated by Paco Sordo

ISLE OF MISFITS

FIRST CLASS

BOOK 1

by JAMIE MAE
illustrated by FREYA HARTAS

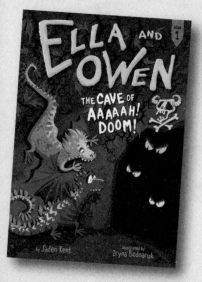

ELLA AND OWEN

BOOK 1

THE CAVE OF AAAAAH! DOOM!

by Jaden Kent
Illustrated by Iryna Bodnaruk

Mighty MEG

BOOK 1

and the Magical Ring

BY Sammy Griffin
Illustrated by Micah Player

Read on for a sneak peek from the second book in the **MONSTER AND ME** series.

Chapter 1:
Orange You Glad
You Came To the Festival?

Freddy von Frankenstein was on a secret mission. He lived high up in the Himalaya Mountains, in a country called Nepal. Today he snuck into the town at the foot of the mountains with a giddy smile. The townspeople were celebrating the most exciting event in Nepal . . . the Biska Jatra festival!

All the townspeople were celebrating the new year with music and dancing. But Freddy thought the most fun part was that they flung a bright, red-orange powder called "sindoor" at each other. Everyone was covered in orange! This special day, called Sindoor Jatra, is celebrated like this every year.

Freddy had watched the festival from the top of the mountain for years. And this time, he was determined to join the fun. Freddy shouted, "Time to get splattered!" as he ran into the crowd to get covered in sindoor. But just then, he heard the sound of *Bzzzt bzzzt!* He was getting a surprise video call on his wrist communicator.

"Bummer," moaned Freddy. He wanted to ignore it and continue celebrating, but the call was from his brother and best friend, F.M., so he answered.

"Where are you?!" his big brother asked.

"I'm down in the village about to get covered head to toe in orange stuff!" said Freddy.

F.M. looked worried. "Freddy, you're not supposed to go down to the village alone. You're gonna get in trouble!"

Freddy laughed and said, "Come down and join in, and then I won't be alone. And you can have a good time getting splattered too! Pleeeease. You don't want me to get into trouble, do you?"

Freddy was usually pretty good at convincing F.M. to go along with his schemes. But not this time! Hanging out in a crowd of humans was just about the scariest thing F.M. could imagine. When he was created by Freddy's dad, Victor, the local villagers were terrified. They chased Victor and F.M. out of town, and F.M. has been afraid of people ever since.

So F.M. quickly changed the subject. "But Mom is looking for you! You're behind on your chores,

so you'd better zoom back up to the palace before she learns you've snuck out. Riya and I are already half-done with ours!"

Freddy groaned with disappointment. Having a brother and sister who always did the right thing was no fun. He hopped on his super-cycle and raced up the mountain, using the turbo boost to make it back in record time.

Cort Lane is a producer, creative exec, and storyteller with two decades of kids' television experience at Marvel/Disney and Mattel. He has credits on over 50 productions, two Emmy nominations, and two NAACP Image Nominations. He currently serves on GLAAD's Kids and Family Advisory Council, and is working on the new *My Little Pony* series on Netflix.

Ankitha Kini is an animator, comics artist, and illustrator. She loves stories steeped in culture and history. A mix of whimsy, fact, and fantasy brings life to her creature-filled world. When she's not drawing, she likes to travel and to make friends with stray cats. She studied Animation Film Design at NID in Ahmedabad, India, and now lives in Eindhoven, the Netherlands.

ankithakini.com